Desmond Gets Free

by Matt Meyer
illustrated by Khim Fam

Published by Skinner House Books, an imprint of the Unitarian Universalist Association, 24 Farnsworth St., Boston, MA 02210–1409.

skinnerhouse.org

Printed in the United States

Illustrations by Khim Fam
Design by Tim Holtz

print ISBN: 978-1-55896-905-6
eBook ISBN: 978-1-55896-867-7

5 4 3 2 1
26 25 24 23

CIP information is on file with the Library of Congress.

For all those working
to build a new world
of justice, equity,
and compassion.

Desmond the mouse
lived in the most beautiful
meadow in all the land.

Every morning, Desmond woke
with the sunrise and would spend
the day playing in the meadow.

And every evening, Desmond would go to sleep in the middle of that meadow under the beautiful starry sky.

One night though, Desmond awoke when it was still dark out. He tried to roll over to a more comfortable spot, but something wasn't right.

Desmond realized that his tail was stuck right to the ground and beginning to throb with pain. He felt behind him and there was a HUGE boulder that seemed to have fallen in the middle of the meadow, just on his tail.

Desmond pushed on the
boulder and tugged on his tail.

He pushed on the boulder and
tugged on his tail!

And he pushed and tugged
and pushed and tugged!

But it was no use.

When he was out of
breath and had just about
given up, he saw a giraffe
nearby in the grass.

"Good news," he thought!

"Oh Giraffe," Desmond cried, "Could you please push the boulder a few inches in the other direction so that I could go free?"

The giraffe looked at Desmond and laughed the way giraffes do.

"Silly Mouse," said the giraffe, "That's no boulder! That's an elephant that's fallen asleep in the middle of the meadow, just on your tail."

"Well, if you could just wake the elephant and ask him to roll over just a few inches in the other direction, I could go free!"

"Well," replied the giraffe, "you know what they say about letting sleeping elephants lie. I find it's best not to get involved in other animals' business. I find it's best to remain neutral in times like this."

Desmond quietly replied, "Well, I do not appreciate your neutrality."

The giraffe wandered off and Desmond tried calling out to the elephant to wake him up. But those giant ears were just too far away on the other side of that giant elephant body.

So again, Desmond pushed on the elephant and tugged on his tail.

He pushed and he tugged and he pushed and he tugged.

But it was no use.

When he was out of breath and had just about given up again, a gazelle wandered by.

"Oh Gazelle," he cried!
"Oh Gazelle! It seems
that an elephant has
fallen asleep just on
my tail in the middle
of this meadow.
I'm stuck and it *hurts*!

I wonder if you could gently wake him and ask him to roll over just a few inches in the other direction, so I might go free."

"Well," said the gazelle, "I see your problem there, but you know what they say about letting sleeping elephants lie. I find it's best not to get involved in other animals' business. I find it's best to remain neutral in times like these."

Desmond replied, almost to himself this time, “I do not appreciate your neutrality.”

Desmond tried
again to call out
to the elephant.

He tried again
to push the giant
animal away.

He tried again
and again to tug
his little tail free,
but it was no use.

When he was out of breath and had just about given up for the last time, he saw another mouse wandering through the meadow.

"My name is Nelson."

"Nelson, this giant elephant has fallen asleep just on my tail in the middle of this meadow. I wonder if you might run over and call out into his giant ears and ask him to roll over just a few inches in the other direction, so I could go free," Desmond asked.

"Of course!" said Nelson.

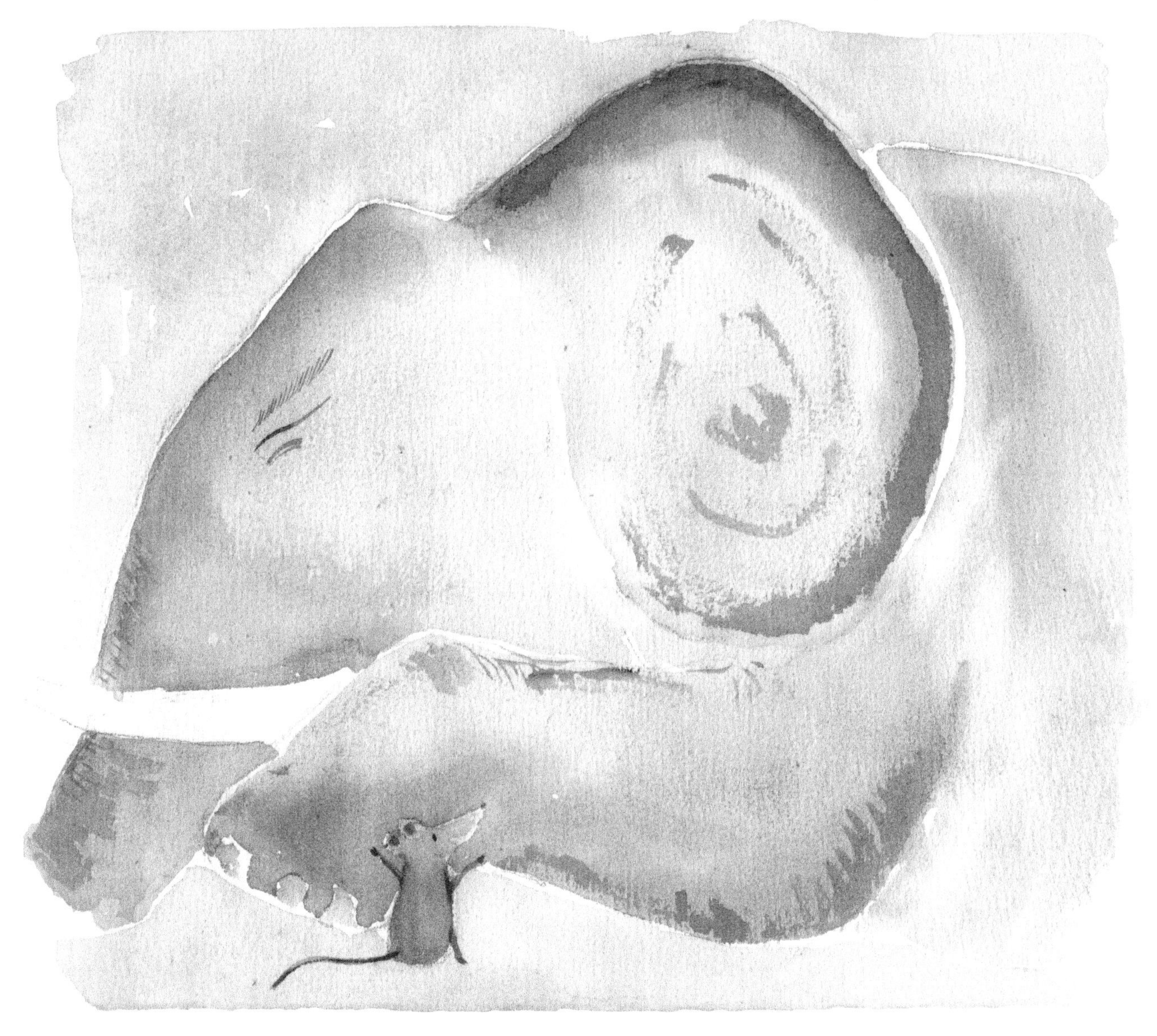

Nelson ran all the way to the other end of that giant elephant body and he called up to those giant elephant ears at the top of that giant elephant head. But the elephant didn't budge. The elephant heard Nelson's small voice far away, but he felt too comfortable to move.

Nelson ran back to Desmond,
a little out of breath, and
said, "I have an idea.
Don't move!"
He ran off.

"I won't," muttered
Desmond.

A little while later though, Nelson emerged through the tall grass and he wasn't alone! Nelson had found three other mouse friends to help him and each one of them had also brought another three friends.

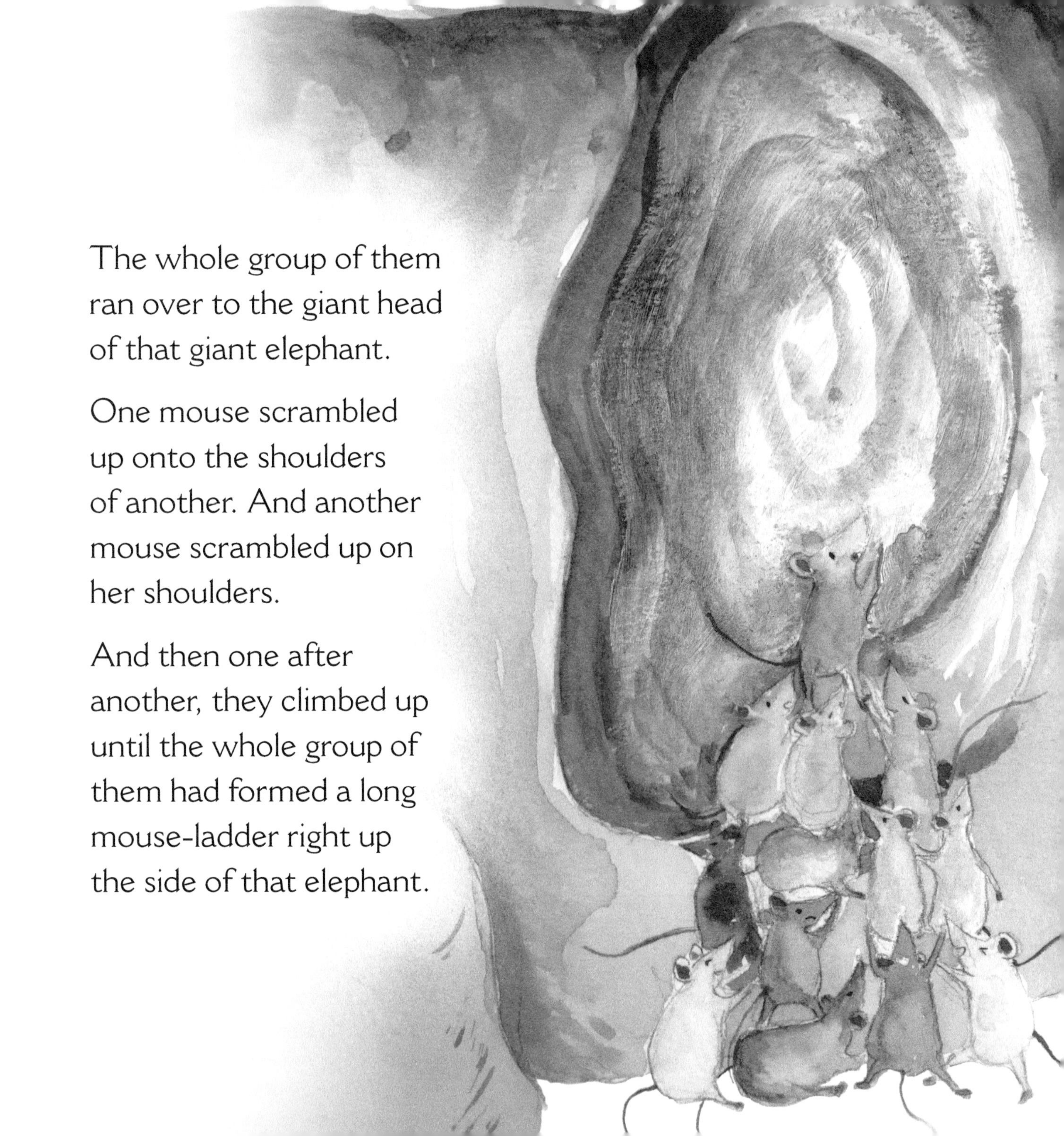

The whole group of them ran over to the giant head of that giant elephant.

One mouse scrambled up onto the shoulders of another. And another mouse scrambled up on her shoulders.

And then one after another, they climbed up until the whole group of them had formed a long mouse-ladder right up the side of that elephant.

At last, Nelson climbed up the shoulders of his mouse friends, one on top of the other, until he was way up on that giant elephant head standing next to that giant elephant ear.

"Excuse me," he called out right
into that ear, "it seems you've
fallen asleep on my friend's tail
in the middle of this meadow.
I wonder if you could just roll
over a few inches in the
other direction, so he
might go free!"

The giant elephant made a giant low groan, "grumpf."

"I'm comfortable just where I am. Go away!"

So Nelson asked more of his mouse friends to climb up.
One by one they helped each other up the side of the elephant.
One by one they called out into that giant elephant ear on top of that giant elephant head.

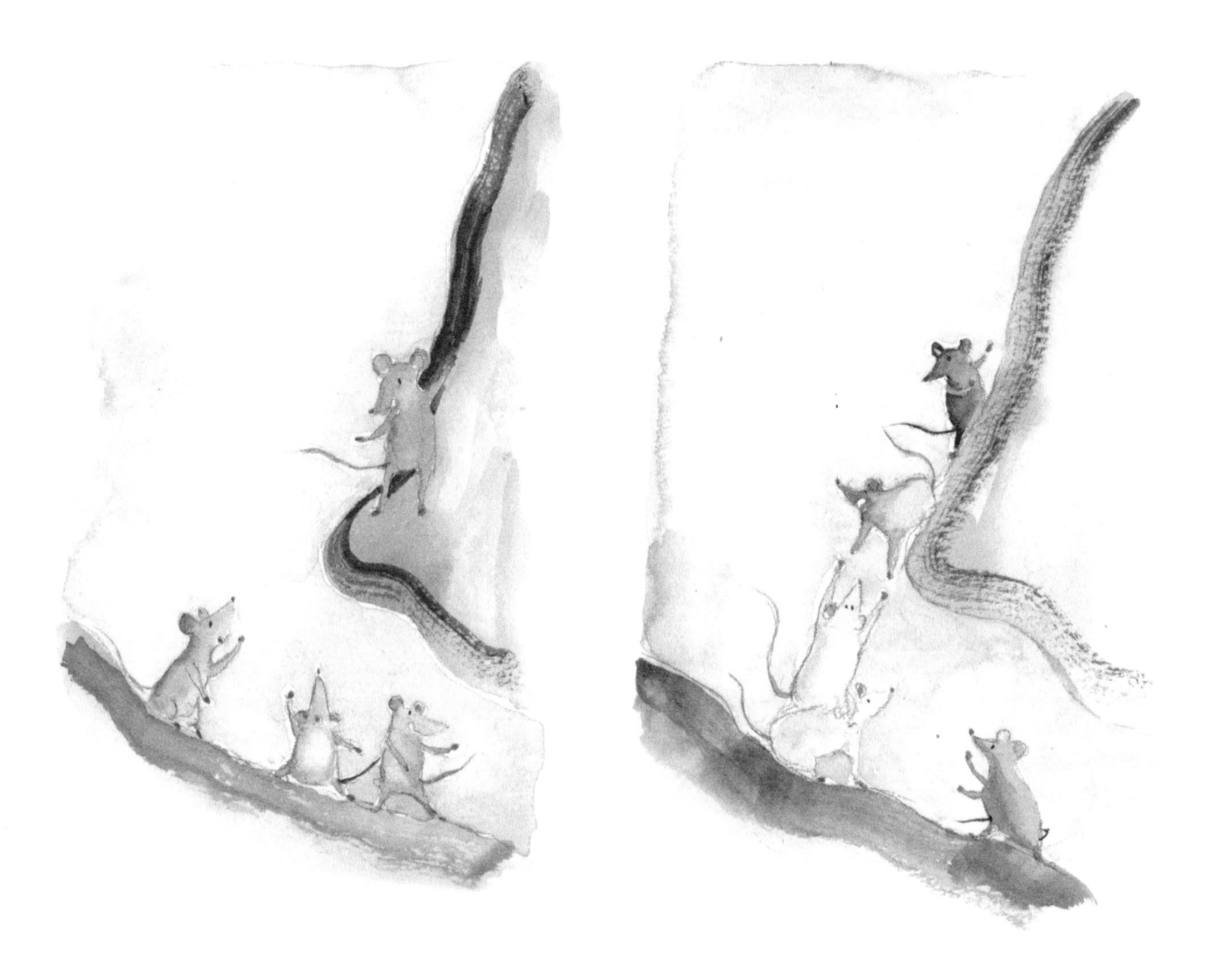

Again the giant elephant made a giant low groan, "grrrrumpf."

"I'm comfortable just where I am! Go away!"

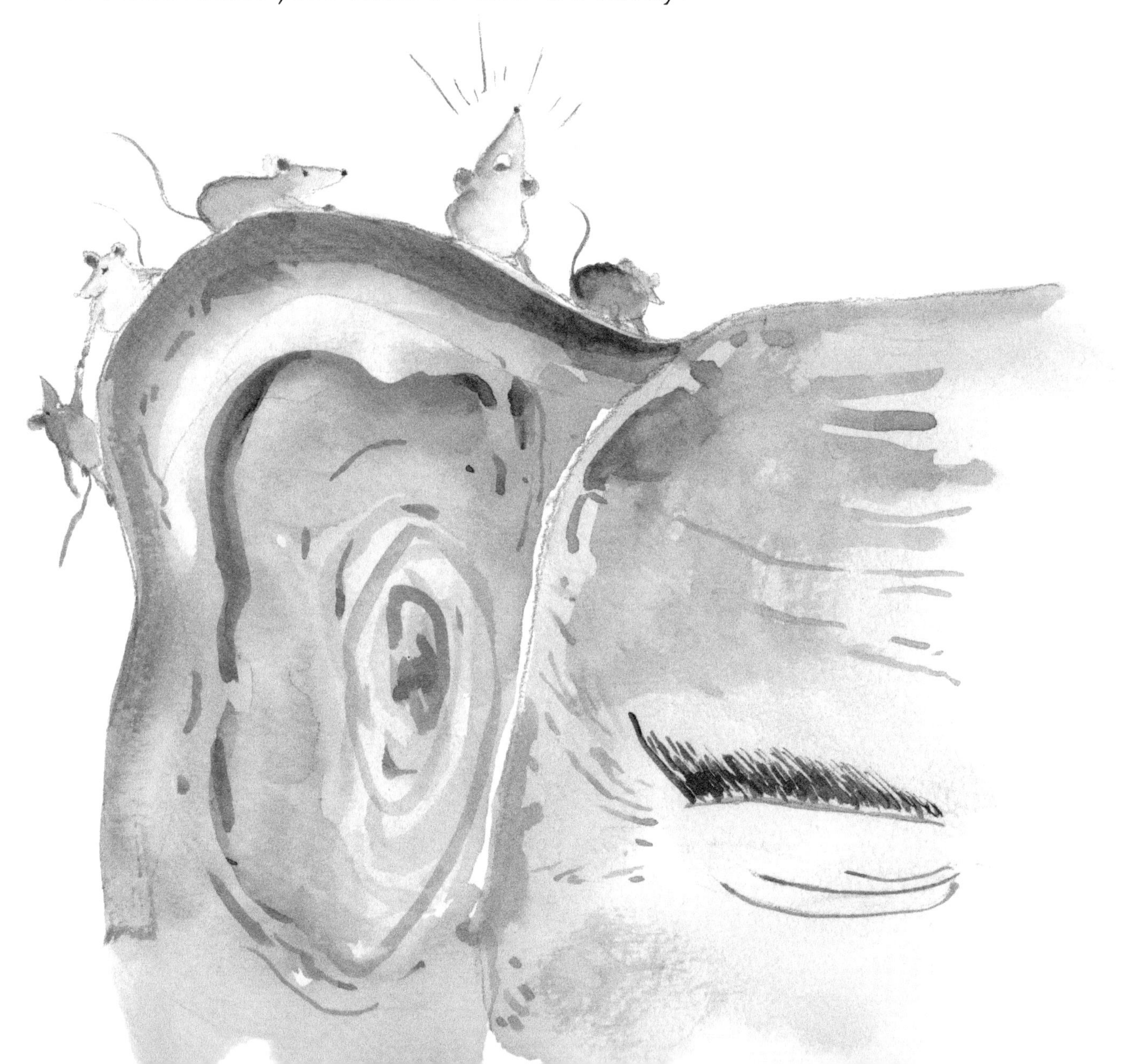

Then Nelson had an idea. He whispered to the mice and then all at once they yelled out together,

"EXCUSE US, it seems you've fallen asleep on our friend's tail in the middle of this meadow! Roll over a few inches in the other direction, so he can go free!"

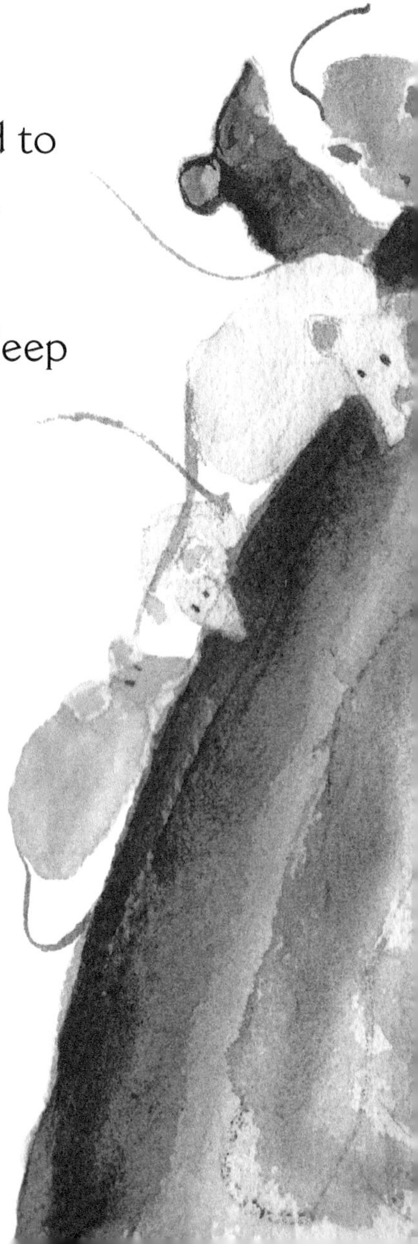

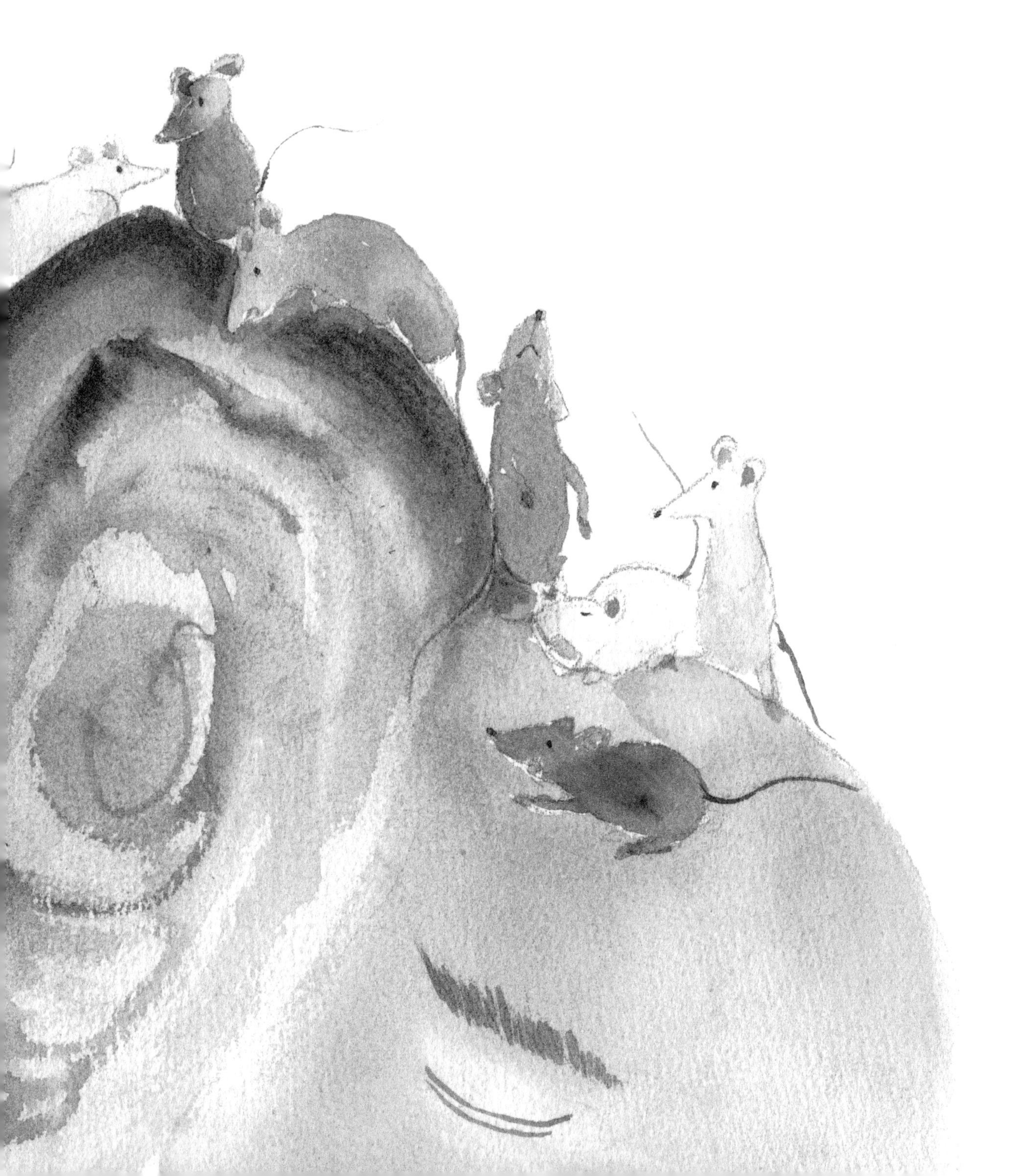

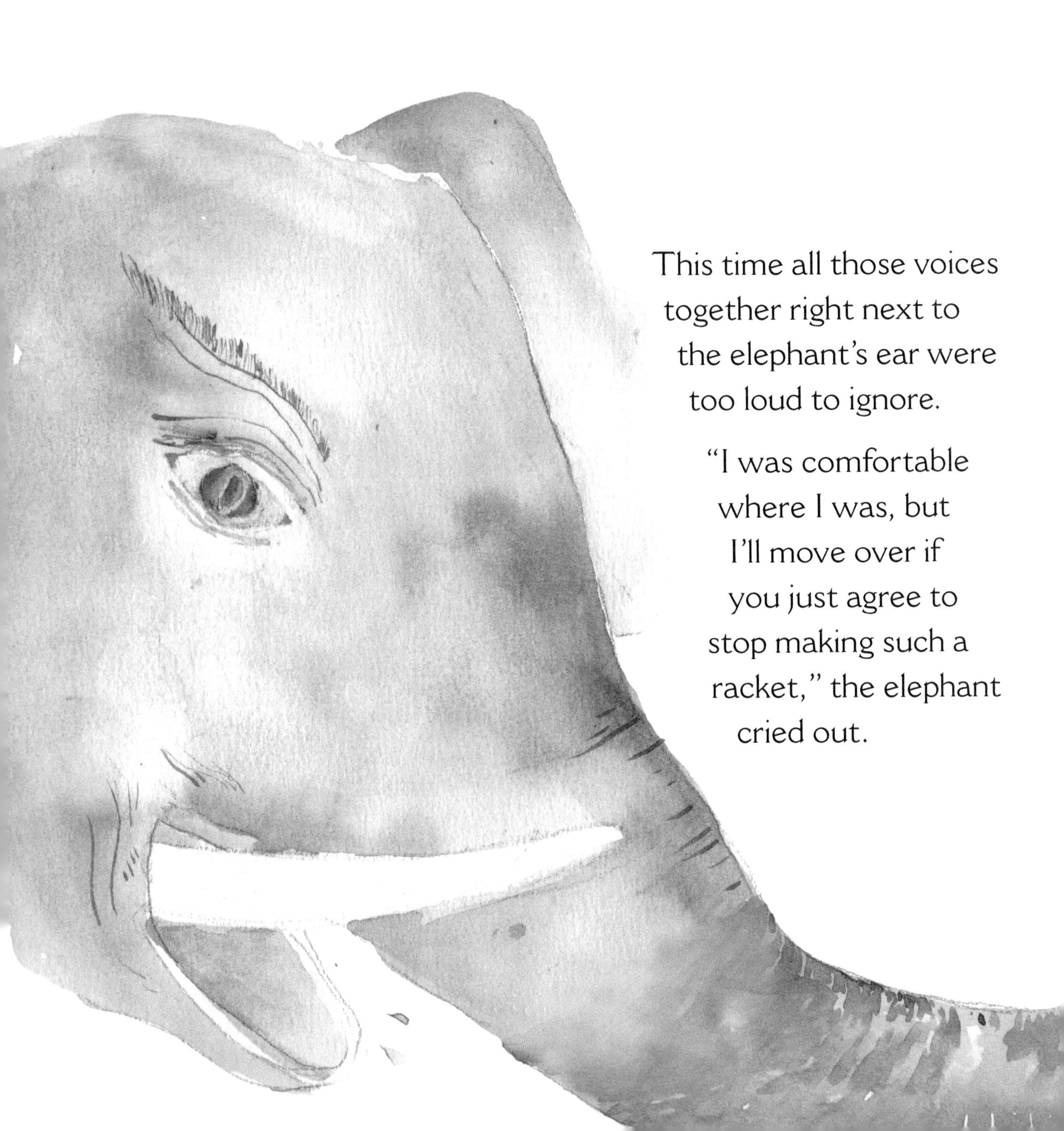

This time all those voices together right next to the elephant's ear were too loud to ignore.

"I was comfortable where I was, but I'll move over if you just agree to stop making such a racket," the elephant cried out.

And then the elephant rolled over just a few inches in the other direction.

Nelson and the other mice helped each other climb back down and Desmond was finally free.

Desmond and Nelson and all their mouse friends spent the rest of that beautiful day playing in the middle of that beautiful meadow.

"If you are neutral in situations of injustice, you have chosen the side of the oppressor. If an elephant has its foot on the tail of a mouse and you say that you are neutral, the mouse will not appreciate your neutrality."

—Archbishop Desmond Tutu

Desmond Mpilo Tutu (born October 7, 1931, died December 26, 2021) was a South African Anglican cleric and theologian who received the Nobel Peace Prize in 1984 for his work as an anti-apartheid and human rights activist. He was the Bishop of Johannesburg from 1985 to 1986 and then the Archbishop of Cape Town from 1986 to 1996. In both cases, he was the first Black African to hold the position.